OUR
BIG
BLUE
SOFA

D0767664

THINGS
FOUND
(LAST YEAR)
UNDER THE
CUSHIONS OF
OUR BIG
BLUE SOFA

A pizza crust

The letter G from
the word game
Scrabble

The instructions
for the
video player

Mum's car keys

A newsletter
from school

A mountain of
biscuit crumbs

Granny Clayton's
bus pass

A dead fly

A moth's wing

The Joker from a
pack of cards

A golf ball

Dad's reading
glasses

Dad's case for his
reading glasses

A phone bill

Pine needles
from last year's
Christmas tree

2 pieces of
red Lego

A shopping list

A tie –
probably Dad's

A dirty teaspoon

A postcard from
Granny Clayton

Two biros

A pink paperclip

A knitting needle

Binky's
cat collar

A blue button

£100
of Monopoly
money

A pea

If found, please return this book to the sofa.

For Wanda, Ava and Bill
with love

In memory of Irene

I would like to thank
Celia Catchpole and
Emma Harris for
their support and
encouragement.

FOUND
UNDER THE
CUSHIONS OF
OUR BIG
BLUE SOFA

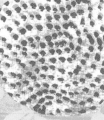

Fossilised Crisp
[Actual Size]

First published 2006 by Macmillan Children's Books
This edition published 2018 by Macmillan Children's Books
an imprint of Pan Macmillan,
20 New Wharf Road, London N1 9RR
Associated companies throughout the world
www.panmacmillan.com

ISBN: 978-1-5290-0590-5

Text and illustrations copyright © Tim Hopgood 2006, 2015
Moral rights asserted.

All rights reserved. No part of this publication may be reproduced, stored in
or introduced into a retrieval system, or transmitted, in any form, or by any means
(electronic, mechanical, photocopying, recording or otherwise) without the prior written
permission of the publisher. Any person who does any unauthorized act in relation to this
publication may be liable to criminal prosecution and civil claims for damages.

1 3 5 7 9 8 6 4 2

A CIP catalogue record for this book is available from the British Library.

Printed in China

OUR
BIG
BLUE
SOFA

tim hopgood

MACMILLAN CHILDREN'S BOOKS

Our sofa is big and blue. It's been in our family for years.
No one knows exactly how old it is, but I reckon it's older than my Dad and he's older than anyone else I know – apart from Granny Clayton, and she's nearly a 100!

This is me.
My name is
Jessica,
but everyone
calls me Jessy.

And this is my
brother Tom.

One of our favourite things is bouncing
on our **big blue sofa.**

"Stop that
at once!"

says Mum.

"Sofas are for sitting on
and NOT
for bouncing!"

"We're practising for the Sofa Bouncing World
Championships!" we explain.

Dad says,
"That sofa's had it!
It's lumpier
than ever!"

But our two cats Inky and Binky don't seem to mind. And neither do we. We have great adventures on our big blue sofa.

Today Tom and I are explorers on a
big blue submarine.

"Has ANYONE seen the remote control for the TV?" asks Dad.

"It's at the bottom of the ocean," I reply.
"But watch out for the sharks!"

NEE- NAR!

NEE- NAR!

Emergency! Here comes the
big blue hospital bed.

I'm busy treating patients for broken bones and infectious diseases.

Granny Clayton says that the big blue sofa is terrible for her bad back. She says she knows a place where Mum and Dad can buy a not-quite-perfect sofa for less than half-price. But why would we want a not-quite-perfect sofa when we already have a big blue sofa that is absolutely perfect?

Today it's a

big blue hot air balloon

and we're flying high above the clouds.

Dad asks,

"Why are the cushions **all over the floor?**"

"They're not cushions, they're sandbags," says Tom.

Mum says,

"Well please **tidy up the sandbags** before tea."

Mum is calling
from the other
room,

"TOM! JESSY!
Tea's ready."

We can only just hear her because now we're in
a **big blue taxicab**

and we're stuck in traffic on a noisy city street.

After tea, Dad says,

"Come along you two.

It's time for bed!"

But we're riding through the jungle on the back of a big blue elephant.

"Can we stay
up?" asks Tom.
"Elephants don't
like to be rushed."

"Ten more minutes
and then
straight
to bed,"
says Dad.

Disaster!

This morning something
awful happened!

While Tom was trying to beat his own World
Record for non-stop bouncing, there was a huge
thud and the whole room shook.

Our **big blue sofa** isn't bouncy any more.

"Is our sofa going to be mended?" I ask Mum. She says that she's ordered a new one. But I don't want a new one.

"I want our big blue sofa," I say. "So do I!" says Tom

Our big blue sofa is missing!

There's just a

big dusty space

where it should be.

Wow!

Look at our
**brand
new
sofa!**

"Don't forget,
NO bouncing
on the brand
new sofa,"
says Mum.

It's huge!
It's so big that
it makes the
cats look like
kittens again.

Our **brand new sofa** is so big, there's enough room on it for all our friends. Granny Clayton says we've probably broken a World Record for the-most-friends-on-a-sofa-at-any-one-time.

And best of all . . .

. . . every now and
then, when no one's
looking, it makes a
fantastic trampoline.

We're busy practising for the

Sofa Olympics!

"TOM! JESSY!
Stop bouncing!"

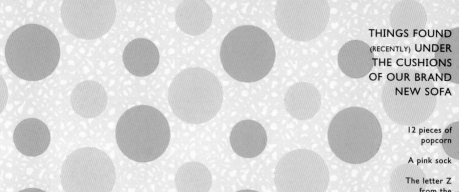

THINGS FOUND (RECENTLY) UNDER THE CUSHIONS OF OUR BRAND NEW SOFA

12 pieces of popcorn

A pink sock

The letter Z from the word game SCRABBLE

The instructions for the DVD player

Mum's car keys

Dad's reading glasses

Dad's case for his reading glasses

Found anything interesting under your sofa's cushions?

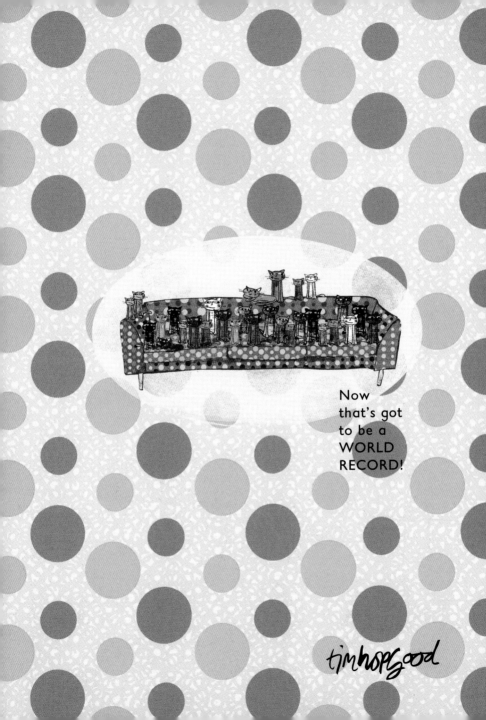

Now
that's got
to be a
WORLD
RECORD!

tim hopgood